Steer Clear

STEER CLEAR

A Christian Guide to Teen Temptations

Kathleen Winkler

CPH.
SAINT LOUIS

*To the faculty of the Graduate School
of Journalism at Marquette University,
especially Dr. Robert Griffin, with thanks
for your wisdom, encouragement,
and support*

Copyright © 1997 Concordia Publishing House
3558 S. Jefferson Avenue, St. Louis, MO 63118-3968
Manufactured in the United States of America

Library of Congress Cataloging-in-Publication Data

Winkler, Kathleen.
    Steer clear: a Christian guide to teen temptations / Kathleen Winkler.
        p.   cm.
    Summary: Describes the experiences of a number of teens who have faced the consequences of such risky behavior as using drugs or alcohol, engaging in premarital sex, and giving into peer pressure to emphasize the importance of avoiding these temptations.
    ISBN 0-570-04957-1
    1. Teenagers—United States—Religious life. 2. Teenagers—United States—Conduct of life. 3. Temptation—Juvenile literature.
    [1. Temptation. 2. Christian life. 3. Conduct of life.]
    I. Title.
    BV4528.2.W56   1997
    248.8'3—dc20   96-41165

1 2 3 4 5 6 7 8 9 10   06 05 04 03 02 01 00 99 98 97

Contents

As You Begin

Dr. James Dobson, a Christian family counselor, once described the teen years as a trip down a hallway lined with doors. Behind each door lurks a temptation: drugs, alcohol, sex outside of marriage, and many others. Those doors, he says, used to be open only a crack. Today they've been taken off their hinges!

As you move into your teen years, to high school and beyond, you will walk down that hallway. The temptations will glitter and sparkle from all sides. You will have to choose whether to walk into the rooms, or, with God's help, to resist and walk straight down the hallway.

The doors don't carry signs that warn you of the consequences of the temptations. These consequences can change your life in an instant—in a crash of grinding metal after drinking and driving; in the cry of your baby born when you are still a child; in the pain of a sexually transmitted disease.

Just knowing there are temptations isn't enough. You have to know how to resist them. That's what I want to do in this book. I want to let teens who have experienced the consequences share their stories with you. And then these kids—and some experts such as doctors and counselors—will give you practical tips to avoid the temptations and say no.

God has a clear plan for your life. He calls you His child; He loves you. When you do trip up, and we all trip up, remember that you are forgiven because of Jesus. Trust how much He loves you. Never doubt that He'll give you the strength to resist the temptations and make it safely down the hallway.

Kathy Winkler

I

Teen Sex Isn't a Thrill Ride

The first time Jenny had sex, she knew she wasn't in love. A senior in high school, she looked at sex the same way her friends did: It was something everyone did, part of any dating relationship. It was no big deal.

"I knew a lot of girls who were seniors and hadn't done it yet and thought, 'I'm just going to get it out of the way,'" Jenny says. So she drifted into "doing it." After a few months, she and the boy broke up. She tried not to think about it.

During her first semester of college, Jenny started dating a new guy. "I really cared about him," she says. In fact, Jenny thought she was in love this time. Sex became a part of their relationship. After about a year, they broke up too. Besides dealing with the pain of the breakup, Jenny had to deal with the fact that she was pregnant. That story is part of another chapter.

———

Dating and breaking up. Dating someone else and breaking up again. It's a normal part of the teen years. And it's a good part, even though the breakups bring pain. Every time you date a new person you learn something about what guys and girls are like. Each time you learn something about the qualities you want in your future husband or wife.

At least that's the way it's supposed to work. It's part of God's design for you. But too often in today's teen world, something else enters the picture—sex. Too many teens think sex is something you do in *every* dating relationship. They think it's normal.

It's not. As Christians, we know it's not normal because that's what God has told us. He's made it clear that sex, in His plan, is for marriage only. And He had a very good reason for making that rule. It wasn't to cramp your style. It wasn't to pour cold water on your fun. God made that rule because He understands the very basics of human sexuality. After all, He created it.

God understands that when a man and a woman have sex, they share the most intimate moment human beings can enjoy. And with that sharing comes emotional ties. And emotional ties bring consequences—enormous consequences.

Linda McClintock, a psychotherapist who has worked with teens both in groups and in individual counseling, says the biggest emotional consequence of teen sex is a loss of self-esteem. This loss can happen to both sexes but is especially hard for girls. "Girls often say a side of them said, 'I don't think I want to do this,'" says McClintock. "They know they weren't true to that side when they went ahead and had sex."

Many teens have a hard time talking about sex, McClintock admits, even with the person with whom they are most intimate. They end up getting sucked into the heat of the moment. Often decisions are based on the word of friends who say, "Go ahead. I've done it, and it's okay." They aren't true to their own values.

"Almost without exception, the sexually active teens I talk with—boys and girls—say that they wanted to save themselves for the person they would marry. Because they haven't, they feel they've betrayed something important," McClintock says. "That makes them feel bad about themselves."

When the relationship breaks up—let's face it, most teen romances do—both people, but especially the girl, can feel used. "He said he loved me." "He said he'd stay with me forever. Now he's gone." Too many girls say phrases like these through a curtain of tears. Too often these girls feel they were an object, something used for someone else's sexual fun.

Teen sex often brings the emotional reaction of "since I've done it once, I'm no longer saving myself for marriage. What's the difference if I do it again?" The consequence of this emotional reaction is an attitude that can lead teens to have meaningless sex on every casual date. McClintock remembers one girl who had sex with more than 20 guys during high school. The girl called them "bed buddies." Her attitude was "What does it matter? It's just sex."

That, McClintock says, is a real tragedy. "Sex is one of God's gifts. You can't treat it lightly no matter how hard you try. Even though our culture says you can, it's impossible because you're dealing with your conscience," McClintock says. She insists that deep inside, teens who are sexually active know they shouldn't be. "God gave us a conscience," she explains. "Even if everyone around you is doing it, you know it's wrong." That conflict, even if it's buried deep, eventually causes problems.

There are other emotional consequences too. Sex usually destroys friendships. "Teens tell me that if you've had sex, it's really hard to see that person after the relationship is over. It's difficult to look him or her in the eye," McClintock says. Many times the partner who has been "dumped" nurses a hatred as he or she sees the "ex" moving on to the next relationship, especially if it's sexual too.

And you have to consider your reputation. While teen sex seems more acceptable than it was years ago, it's a mistake to think that no one cares or pays attention. Kids still get a reputation among their peers. A reputation as "easy" or "a user" develops fast and becomes hard to shake.

McClintock has a special word for guys, who are often ignored when discussing the consequences of teen sex. "I don't think many guys understand the emotional side of having sex," she says. "Their hormones are doing their thinking!"

"Guys, you need to ask, 'Am I ready for this girl to form an emotional attachment to me?' When you have sex, the girl will have feelings for you," McClintock explains. "Are you ready to face the consequences of that attachment?" Not to mention the consequences of your emotional attachment to the girl.

It takes a great deal of courage for a guy to resist peer pressure to "prove" he's a man by having sex. It takes much more maturity to say no than to follow the crowd. It's what God calls guys to do.

———

Looking back, Jenny says she thinks becoming sexually active too young takes a huge emotional toll. "You can't say it doesn't have any effect, especially when you are no longer with that person," Jenny says. "It has an effect. It takes something away from you."

That "something" Jenny refers to is self-esteem and self-respect. It's living in harmony with God's will. It's living with the understanding that you are "fearfully and wonderfully made" by God. It's knowing that He sent His Son, Jesus, to die for your mistakes. God's love is the core of your self-esteem. You have value because He loves you.

Living in harmony with God's will is not something to be thrown away. It's how you avoid emotional earthquakes. And remember, you don't have to do it alone. Through the Holy Spirit, God provides strength and encouragement. That's part of His plan too.

2 ◈

Caution: Baby on Board

Jenny, the young woman in the last chapter, understands firsthand one of the results of sex. During her first semester of college, just after she and her boyfriend broke up, Jenny learned she was pregnant. The day the doctor told her, she sat in his office and cried.

Eventually Jenny had to go home to her mother. Jenny's parents had been divorced for years, and she had little contact with her father. "I was scared to tell anyone," she says. "I never thought my mother would 'kill me' or anything like that, but we were pretty close. I was afraid this was something she'd take on herself. I didn't want to put her through it."

But Jenny sat down with her mother and choked out the words, "I'm pregnant." Her mother started crying; so did Jenny. First, they hugged while they cried. Then they asked the question all pregnant teenagers and their families have to ask: "What are we going to do?"

"I knew abortion wasn't a choice for me," Jenny says. That left two options: keeping the baby or giving it up for adoption. "There was never any doubt in my mind that I would keep the baby," she remembers. "I could never give him up."

So Jenny set out on the long, difficult road of parenthood. Because she didn't want to marry the baby's father, she walked it alone.

Motherhood had a huge impact on Jenny's life. "As hard as you might imagine it would be to raise a child in your teens, it's at least 10 times harder," Jenny says. "It feels like your life has been taken away from you because you have to do somebody else's. There's no way your life is going to be the same, no matter how much you think it will be."

Jenny points to a string of changes her child has brought to her life.

- *She's way behind where she should be in school.* Jenny's friends have graduated from college. She's only a sophomore.

- *Her social life has changed.* "It's hard when people call at the last minute and say, 'Hey, you want to go do this or that,'" Jenny says. "I can't do a lot of things. People don't realize I have to get a baby-sitter and be home at a certain time."

- *It's affected her dating.* "You wonder if any guy will want to go out with you again because you have a kid," Jenny says. "It's weird when I meet someone—having to say I have a son."

- *She's afraid to form a close relationship with a guy.* Jenny doesn't want her son to become attached to someone because if they break up, he would lose someone too.

- *Financially, it's incredibly tight.* Jenny's going to school and working 20 hours a week. "I have to put my son first," she says. "Even if I plan to buy something for myself, when I get to the store, I end up buying stuff for him."

Then there are all the little things Jenny says she never thought of before her son was born: She can't sleep late because she has to fix breakfast for him. She has to make him dinner every night. She can't just veg out—he's always there, wanting attention. She has to get up with him in the middle of the night—every night—because he doesn't sleep through the night yet. Once he pulled the plug on the computer, and Jenny lost a term paper the night before it was due.

The burden has fallen almost entirely on Jenny because her baby's father lives in another part of the state. He isn't involved with his child. "I wouldn't give him the 'Father of the Year' award," Jenny says.

Yet as hard as it is, Jenny wants to make it clear that she loves her little boy. "Whenever I get really frustrated, I just sit down and watch him—he's the greatest thing!" she says. Great kid but too soon.

———

A girl who becomes pregnant outside of marriage doesn't have any good choices, says Linda McClintock. If you believe what God says about the value of life, abortion is not an option. Some young women, however, are pressured into an abortion by others who see it as the "best choice." If you make that decision, you may regret it later. You may feel guilty. You need to hear God's message of forgiveness. If you are the young man who is equally responsible for the pregnancy, you may suffer the same guilt—

although many guys deny it and bury it deep inside.

According to McClintock, giving up a baby for adoption is often the best choice for teenage parents. Life in a loving Christian home with two adult parents may be better for the child than being raised by a single teenage mother, especially if the father doesn't hang around. "But adoption brings extreme sadness that each girl has to wrestle with," McClintock says. "Carrying a baby in your body is a bonding process. You have a relationship with that child, and adoption is a painful separation. You may need a lot of counseling to work through it."

Keeping the baby is the third option, and as Jenny has shared, it's not easy. "If you are a kid raising a kid, it's a tremendous responsibility," McClintock says. "There's a high risk for child abuse or neglect, especially with very young teen parents."

Jenny was fortunate that her pregnancy went well, and she and her child are healthy. Some of the youngest teen mothers aren't so lucky. Dr. Debra Schaeffer, an obstetrician-gynecologist, has seen many young teen mothers develop problems. Because the pelvis of girls in their early teens isn't as well-developed, they have a higher rate of cesarean—or C-section—deliveries. In a cesarean, the baby is delivered through an incision into the walls of the abdomen. Schaeffer points out that there's an unexplained higher risk of birth defects in babies born to mothers under age 15.

While the teen mother may have the worst of the deal, it can be hard for the fathers too. McClintock says many young men carry a deep sense of shame because they aren't standing by their child. Some stay in contact for a while, but when the going gets hard, it's tempting to walk away. "The young father wants to get on with his life. Maybe he has a new girlfriend," McClintock says. "Even though he's supposed to take the baby on weekends, he doesn't. It becomes so easy for him to think, 'I don't have to take this responsibility.' "

If you father a baby, you need to know that the courts can order you to support it. You will pay a percentage of your income until your child is 18. If you don't pay, you are looking at jail time.

———

Jenny still isn't sure why she became sexually active so young. It was partly curiosity, she says, partly her perception that it was what everyone did. She felt that sex was no big deal. Although Jenny was raised in a Christian home, she says God's "don'ts" were not very important to her. "I never saw it as an important part of being a Christian. I just sort of ignored it," Jenny admits. Now that she's a mother, she's much stronger in her faith. "Being pregnant clears up any doubt that there's a God. At least it did for me," she says.

As Jenny reflected on her experience, she offers this advice: "I think it's a good idea to wait for sex. It's not like my life is gone now, but it's completely changed. You have to think about whether you are ready to give up your life and put someone else's life before yours. And don't think about it after you are pregnant. Think about it before."

One of the reasons God tells us that sex belongs in marriage is revealed in the consequences Jenny has suffered. God knows what's best for us and has set up His plan for sex for that reason. His plan is that a child should have a mother and father in the same home and that parents should be together to help each other raise their children.

Following God's plan is the best way to avoid the upheaval of teenage parenthood, raising a child while you're trying to grow up yourself. But God's plan includes His love for you. That means He won't leave you alone—when you're making decisions about sex or when you're living with the consequences of a wrong decision. He will give you strength, and He will forgive. Seek His help in prayer.

3

Accident with Fatalities

Marty was only 17 when she got pregnant. She had grown up in a super-strict home. Because she didn't like her parents' rules, Marty got a job and an apartment and started a new life as soon as she graduated from high school. "It was like I was saying, 'Now I'm out of the house, and I want it all—and in five days or less!' " she remembers. "I wanted everything—drinking and partying included."

Marty's new life included a young man, Simon, who soon moved in with her. Six months later, she was pregnant. "We never thought it would happen to us," she says. Simon didn't want to get married, and he didn't want to become a father either. "I thought having sex and living together were a commitment," Marty says, "but he didn't."

At that time abortion wasn't legal in the United States. Marty found out that if a psychiatrist said she was too mentally unstable to have a baby, an abortion would be legal.

It took a long time to arrange the diagnosis. By the time Marty got everything done, it was too late for an abortion the usual way—sucking the fetus out with a vacuum tube. Marty had to have a saline abortion in which the doctor injects a salt solution into the uterus, killing the fetus. Later, the woman goes into labor and delivers a dead baby.

Marty checked into what she calls the "hospital ward from hell." There were eight or 10 women, all having saline abortions. Their beds were separated by white curtains. Marty lay alone, in labor, for 12 hours before she finally delivered her baby. A nurse hurried in, dropped him into a metal container, and whisked him away—but not before Marty saw him. It's a sight she can't forget.

Marty's also never forgotten what happened next. Even though her abortion had been performed in a hospital, she got a bad infection that spread throughout her body. She needed surgery twice, and at one point she was close to death. When she left the hospital a month later, Marty was weak and thin.

The experience had caused her—and Simon—to become more mature. Within a few months they got married. Everything went well until they decided to start a family. Nothing happened. After months of trying to get pregnant, Marty's doctor told her that scar tissue from the infection had damaged her reproductive organs. She would never be able to have a baby. The news devastated Marty.

"The guilt that I felt—guilt that I'd killed my *only* child—was so bad," Marty says. "What kind of person was I to have allowed such a terrible thing to happen?"

It took Marty and Simon a long time to accept that God, through Jesus Christ, forgives any sin, including the sin of abortion. When they finally accepted His forgiveness, they felt as if a weight had been lifted from their hearts. Even though the guilt was gone, the sadness remained. Nothing could undo the terrible effect of the abortion.

"Abortion is a lifelong decision," says Mary Zutavern, a counselor with PACE (Post-Abortion

Counseling and Education), a Christian counseling program. For years, Zutavern's been running groups for women who regret their abortions. Many who come to her groups are teenagers—or were when they had their abortions.

Women who have an abortion run a lot of emotional risks, Zutavern says. The problems she sees most often are

- *Guilt.* When a woman realizes she took the life of her child, even if she was very young and scared at the time, she can feel enormous guilt. Many women say they know that God forgives any sin, but they can't seem to forgive themselves. It may take a lot of counseling before a woman can accept that her sin is gone, washed away by Jesus' death on the cross.

- *Depression.* Women who have had an abortion run a risk of becoming depressed. For most it's a low-level sadness, but a few become deeply depressed. Sometimes they drink or take drugs to numb the pain.

- *Anxiety.* Women can become tense, have frequent headaches, or have a hard time concentrating or sleeping after an abortion. Some become especially troubled around the anniversary of the abortion or the time when the baby would have been born.

- *Other psychological problems.* Zutavern says she's had many young women in her groups with eating disorders—either eating so little they starve (anorexia) or even more common, becoming extremely overweight so men won't be attracted to them. Of course, there are many reasons young women have eating disorders, but because it happens frequently *after* an abortion is one clue to the emotional effect of the procedure.

- *Emotional numbness.* A woman might try not to feel anything too deeply so she won't feel too much pain. That can be hard on future dating relationships or a marriage.

- *Resentment toward the people who urged her to have the abortion.* Whether it's the baby's father or her parents, a woman can resent the people who pressured her to have an abortion, especially if she knew it was wrong or didn't really want to have it. Dating relationships usually break up very quickly after an abortion. Relationships with parents can be strained for years.

Men can have the same problems, although they are more likely to put the abortion out of their minds or not realize that their feelings result from a girlfriend's abortion. A male friend, a man now in his 40s, told me he's always been haunted by an abortion a girlfriend had years ago.

Women who have an abortion also run physical risks.

- *Infection.* Marty's abortion was done in a hospital under sterile conditions, but she still got an infection. Women whose abortions are done by unqualified people or who try to bring one on themselves (because they don't want to tell anyone) run a very high risk of infection, bleeding, or damage to their reproductive organs.

- *Future miscarriages.* A woman who has more than one abortion may have a greater risk of losing a baby she wants.

- *Higher risk of breast cancer.* This physical risk isn't a proven fact yet, but several studies indicate that an abortion of a first pregnancy increases the risk of getting breast cancer later in life.

Many young women have been convinced to have an abortion because they were told it's nothing—no worse than having a tooth pulled. That's not true.

"You can get a tattoo and have it removed later when you are sick of it, but you can never go back and remove an abortion," says Zutavern. "You'll always wonder at different stages of your life, especially if you have children later, about that other baby. It can be like a phantom child."

———

God gave women the special gift of having babies. He wants us to love and nurture them. The best way to avoid the abortion decision is to save sex for marriage. If everyone followed God's plan for sex, abortion wouldn't exist, and all the problems it brings would vanish too. God knew what He was doing when He set up His plan.

By the way, Marty and Simon finally adopted two little girls from South America. They are a happy family now, although they have never forgotten the little boy who "might have been."

4 ◈
....

Warning: Dangerous Diseases Ahead

I wanted to start every chapter with a teenager telling how he or she handled the issue the chapter discusses, but when it came to discussing sexually transmitted diseases, no one was willing to talk. That says something about what our society thinks about sexually transmitted diseases (STDs).

Most people see STDs as something dirty, something shameful, something that doesn't happen to "nice" people—teens or adults. They are wrong. Even kids and adults who seem clean and not at all "sleazy" can carry an STD. In fact, we have an STD epidemic in America. Statistics from the national Centers for Disease Control say that one out of every four Americans will get an STD sometime between the ages of 15 and 55. Twenty-five percent of sexually active teens will get one before they graduate from high school, which means if you have sex, you've got a one-in-four risk of contracting an STD.

A few years ago, I was part of a group of medical writers that spent time shadowing doctors to find out what their typical day was like. I spent my time with Dr. Evans, a pediatrician. In between checking babies and giving shots, he made a phone call. Here's his side of the conversation.

> Hello, Trish? This is Dr. Evans. I have the results of your test. I hate to tell you this, but you have a sexually transmitted disease. It's called chlamydia. I have to ask if you've had sex lately. Prom night? Well, I know it's going to be hard to do, but you have to call your date and tell him. He probably has it too.

I never met Trish, and I don't know how she reacted, but I can guess. First, she probably cried. Second, she probably took a shower. But you can't wash away an STD. It takes a lot stronger treatment.

Dr. Debra Schaeffer, an obstetrician-gynecologist, says she's seeing more girls with STDs. Her patients are much younger than they used to be. "The youngest used to be 15 or 16, now I'm seeing girls as young as 13 or 14," she says.

Many teenagers are totally unaware of the diseases that can be passed along during sex. (Some diseases also can be spread by sharing the needle of an infected person while using drugs.) Other kids know about STDs but think if they only have sex with "clean" people, they are safe. Still others put their faith in condoms. They've never been told that condoms fail 20 to 40 percent of the time. So much for "safe sex"!

Dr. Schaeffer doesn't want to scare you. She wants you to know about STDs and the bad news about their consequences.

There are more than 20 different infections that can be passed from person to person during sex. Some STDs are caused by bacteria and can be cured with antibiotics. Some are caused by a virus. Because antibiotics don't affect viruses, they can't be cured. Only the symptoms can be treated.

Life often is not fair—while an STD is no picnic for a guy, the consequences for a girl are more severe. Not only can girls be infected more easily than guys, STDs can cause serious problems if they aren't diagnosed and treated.

Many STDs, Dr. Schaeffer explains, can cause pelvic inflammatory disease (PID), which is a raging infection in the uterus, the ovaries, the fallopian tubes, or other abdominal organs. "The infection can cause scars," Dr. Schaeffer says. "The scars can close off the fallopian tubes or prevent the ovaries from making eggs properly. The woman may never be able to have a baby."

We can't cover all STDs and all the problems they cause in one short chapter, but let's take a look at the most common ones.

- *Chlamydia.* This is the most common STD. It's caused by a bacteria that has to live in a human cell so you can get it only from sexual contact. (You don't have to worry about getting it—or most STDs—from dirty bathrooms.) Often there are no symptoms, but sometimes there's a discharge from the vagina or the penis. There also could be burning when urinating and mild pain in the lower abdomen. Chlamydia can cause PID. If a woman gives birth while she's infected, the baby can get pneumonia and eye infections from traveling through the birth canal. Chlamydia can be treated with antibiotics, but some germs are becoming resistant to the medicine, and it's getting harder to cure.

- *Trichomoniasis.* This infection often doesn't cause any symptoms either, especially in guys. But both sexes can have a yellowish, bad-smelling discharge; irritation and itching in the sex organs; and a burning pain when urinating. If a woman with "trich" is pregnant, it can cause her to go into labor early. It's treated with antibiotics taken by mouth or put into the vagina.

- *Gonorrhea.* According to Dr. Schaeffer, people usually know when they have this STD. There's a pus-filled discharge and itching or burning when urinating. Gonorrhea often leads to PID. If a woman has gonorrhea when she gives birth, the baby could be born blind. In guys, gonorrhea can cause the tube that carries urine out of the body through the penis to shrink. The treatment includes stretching the penis with small tubes; it hurts. Gonorrhea usually is treated with penicillin, but some bacteria are becoming resistant to the medicine, and it's getting harder to cure.

- *Human Papilloma Virus (HPV).* This virus causes warts to grow on the sexual organs of guys and girls. The warts can be on the inside or the outside. Doctors think that in some women these warts can lead to cancer of the opening of the uterus. There is no cure for HPV because it's caused by a virus, but the warts can be burned off with a laser or acid or frozen off. If they become precancerous, they may have to be cut out, which can weaken the entrance to the uterus. This weakening may cause a pregnant woman to go into labor early.

- *Genital Herpes*. This STD is also caused by a virus. It causes painful sores in the genital area. After a few weeks, the virus becomes quiet and the sores go away, but another outbreak can flare up at any time. The sores can be treated with an expensive drug, but the infection can't be cured.

- *Syphilis*. It's not true that syphilis is a disease of the past. Dr. Schaeffer says it's on its way back. The first sign of infection is a painless sore on the sex organ that goes away. The infection has only gone "underground," though. A fever, a sore throat, and a rash may come next. People often think they have the flu. In later stages, syphilis causes brain damage, blindness, and finally, death. Most babies born to infected women don't live because they have such bad birth defects. Syphilis can be cured with penicillin, but like so many other infections, the germs are becoming resistant to the drug.

- *Hepatitis B.* About half the people with this disease don't have any symptoms. The other half have a fever, head and muscle aches, tiredness, and nausea. Their eyes and skin turn yellow. Hepatitis B is caused by a virus. Most people get over it on their own, but some people become carriers. That means they can give it to others. They also have a higher risk of developing liver cancer. Babies born to women with this infection can get it and become carriers also.

- *HIV/AIDS.* For a long time, we thought only homosexuals and people who share needles when doing drugs were at risk of getting HIV, the virus that causes AIDS. The truth is that more and more young people are getting it by having sex with an infected person. HIV-positive people can live for many years without symptoms, spreading the disease every time they have sex. Statistics show that 20 percent of the people with AIDS are in their 20s, which means they were infected as teens. Once AIDS develops, it destroys the body's immune system, which normally fights off diseases. Infections that most people can fight off make an AIDS patient extremely ill. Finally, they can no longer fight off the various illnesses and they die. Some drugs help with symptoms, but there is no cure for AIDS. A pregnant woman can give the virus to her baby. Infected babies often live only a few years.

Besides the physical sickness, STDs cause emotional pain, says Linda McClintock. Guys and girls who get an STD often feel ashamed, embarrassed, and dirty. Girls especially worry about permanent damage to their bodies—a very real fear. Most young girls don't like having a doctor examine their sexual organs, but it may be necessary. It's embarrassing for either a guy or a girl to tell the people they've had sex with that they may have given them a disease.

What's the best way to avoid getting an STD? The answer isn't "use a condom" as you've probably heard on TV or in school. Condoms can *reduce* the risk of getting an STD, but they don't *prevent* them. Studies show that condoms fail between 20 and 40 percent of the time. In consumer tests, up to 20 percent leaked. And condoms can break during sex or slip off. Would you get in a car if you knew it had a 40 percent—or even a 20 percent—risk of crashing?

The only way not to get an STD is to follow God's plan for sex. When two people who have never had sex (or used drugs) come together in marriage, their risk of getting an STD is zero, as long as they have sex only with each other and don't use drugs. (Yes, it's true that some people have gotten the AIDS virus or Hepatitis B from blood products, but modern screening methods have reduced that risk to almost nothing.)

Do you see why God's plan for sex is best? In 1 Corinthians 6:18, God says, "He who sins sexually sins against his own body." This same chapter also reminds us that our bodies are temples of the Holy Spirit, purchased and made holy by the death and resurrection of Jesus. "Therefore honor God with your body" (1 Corinthians 6:20).

5 ◈

Don't Yield to Everything You Hear

Just before Jenny, the girl we met in previous chapters, broke up with her boyfriend, she started a unit on human sexuality in a college biology class. The textbook included a chart of the failure rate for condoms in preventing pregnancy and STDs that ranged from 20 percent (if a condom was used correctly, every time) to 60 percent (if it wasn't used correctly or every time).

"That just blew my mind," Jenny says. "A week later I found out I was pregnant. I was shocked because I'd been using condoms all along. In high school health classes, they made me think condoms are a lot more effective than they really are."

———

Let's be clear about one thing—not all school sex education classes are bad. You need to learn the facts about human sexuality. It's best to learn them from your parents, but your school can also be a source of information.

Some school sex education classes, though, teach kids about sex in a way that leaves out values. Educators call these programs "value neutral," which means that they don't take a position on what's right or wrong. Some classes do teach values, even though they say they don't. And the values they teach usually aren't God's values.

Here are some red flags to watch for. If your school's sex education classes say these things, be careful. They aren't what God says.

- *You have the right to make your own decisions about sex and to form your own values. No one, including your parents, has the right to tell you what you should or should not do.* That's nonsense! God has every right to tell you what you should or should not do sexually. He made you. He created sex. He has the right to put His rules on it. Your parents are God's representatives on earth, and they have the right, from Him, to tell you their sexual values. God will help you respect what they say. While many teens *think* they can decide what's best, the fact is if left on their own, teens often make bad decisions about sex. Listen to what God and your parents tell you. They have your best interests at heart.

- *Sexual activity is normal for teens. It's not realistic to expect them not to have sex.* If that's true, then a lot of teenagers have something radically wrong with them. Even though the media make it sound as if "everyone's doing it," the truth is everyone *isn't* doing it. Many teens have the good sense to decide to wait for sex. They have the strength of character to say no to the pressure. Find friends who feel that way and support one another. It will make resisting pressure easier for all of you.

- *It's impossible for people to control their sexual urges, therefore, you can't either.* Nonsense! People aren't animals. They don't have to act on every urge that enters their heads. You will have sexual urges—you wouldn't be human if you didn't—but you don't have to act on them. Ask God to help you control them until the time He says is right. And God will bless your decisions. It's not easy, but it can be done. Plunge into sports, music, drama—whatever keeps you occupied and fills your life with fun. Lots of different activities and interests will leave you with less time to think about sex. Besides, there's plenty of time for sex when you're married.

- *Practice safe sex: Use a condom.* First, God says, "Don't," not "Don't, unless you use a condom." Remember those failure rates: 20 to 40 percent. That's one out of five times at the minimum.

- *Sex tells how compatible you are with a person before you marry him or her.* One textbook used in some school sex education classes asks if you would buy a car without a test drive. Well, God doesn't allow sexual test drives. Period. The rates of teen pregnancy and STD infection show how harmful "test drives" can be.

What should you do if these ideas are in your sex education class or the textbook it uses?

Speak up. Tell your parents. Show them the book. They need to know what you are being taught.

Then, if they don't agree with it, they can go to the school.

Speak up in class. It takes a lot of guts to say, "That's not right." While some kids might laugh at you, a lot will agree and be happy that someone had the courage to say it, even if they didn't.

Call on God for help. He made you and won't leave you. You have the power of prayer—ask for His help to resist the temptations textbooks may present and to be strong if others snicker at your beliefs. Pray day by day, hour by hour, or minute by minute, if you need to.

———

Remember: Values lie under everything we do in the area of sex. Whose values? For Christian teens, it has to be God's values, no matter what the sex education class says.

6

No Right Turn on Red: Just Say No

We've looked at a lot of reasons why sex is harmful for teenagers. God had some good reasons for saying "Don't!" But it's not enough to tell you not to do it. You face enormous pressure to become sexually active—from friends; from movies and from television shows that glamorize it; and from ads that use sex to sell everything from toothpaste to tires. You may be facing the hardest pressure of all—your boyfriend or girlfriend who says, "If you love me, you'll prove it."

You need some effective ways to say no. Here, from experts such as doctors, psychologists, and other teens, are some ways you can say no to the pressure to have sex.

- *Be sure in your own mind that no is the right answer.* Think through what God says about the proper place for sex. Think through all the things you've read in the previous chapters. What would you do if you or your girlfriend were pregnant? How would you tell your boyfriend or girlfriend that you had a sexually transmitted disease? Only when you are perfectly sure that no is the right answer can you say it firmly and confidently enough for the other person to listen.

- *Promise yourself that you won't have sex until marriage.* Maybe it would help to write it down and keep it where you can reread it when you need to. If the temptation is very strong, it might help to post your pledge somewhere in your room where you will see it all the time. If your boyfriend or girlfriend feels the way you do, sign a mutual pledge.

- *Find friends who share your values.* It's especially important to have a close friend, perhaps a best friend, who feels like you do. Then you can talk about temptations and give each other support and encouragement. When the rest of the world is saying you're crazy for waiting, it helps to have a special friend say, "No, you're not crazy. Hang in there."

- *Work on self-esteem and assertiveness skills.* If you truly value yourself, you will know you are worth waiting for. A lot of teens, especially girls, have been brought up to always be polite and go along with things rather than cause trouble. That's not good advice in the area of sex. You have to stand up for yourself and for what you believe, even if it means not being polite. You have the right to your values and to be respected. If you have trouble standing up for yourself, look into an assertiveness training class. It can teach you how to express your opinions and stick to them in ways that others will respect.

- *Carefully choose your dates.* Look for people who share your Christian values. That's not to say sexual temptation won't happen if you're dating a Christian, but it makes it easier if you both feel the same way about waiting for sex.

- *Stay out of situations that create temptation.* Don't

spend hours alone in the house with your boyfriend or girlfriend when your parents are gone—find activities you both enjoy and keep busy. Don't drink. Alcohol numbs your thinking and can make you do things you wouldn't do otherwise. For many teens, sex happens when the partners have been drinking. Be careful how you dress—wearing sexually suggestive clothes can send a message to your date that you are open to sex even if that's not what you mean.

- *Set limits early in a relationship.* Tell the guy or girl you are dating that you are willing to go so far and no further. Remember, if you start "fooling around," it can be hard to stop. Also, your date may think that if sexual touching is okay, then sex must be too.

- *Use the word no over and over.* Linda McClintock calls it the broken record technique. "No doesn't have to have anything else attached to it. It's very effective all by itself," she says. Say it over and over in the same tone of voice. Your date will get pretty tired of asking the question!

- *Don't believe it if your date says there's something wrong with you.* "You must be frigid" or "You're not much of a man" are hard phrases to hear.

Remember, saying no to sex doesn't make them true. Tell the other person, "You're entitled to your opinion, but it's not true." Saying that over and over is better than getting into an argument where you may have to prove something.

- *Put the blame on God or your parents—their shoulders are big enough.* "God says sex before marriage isn't right, and I listen to Him" or "My parents would kill me if I got pregnant or got an STD" can turn off somebody who is pressuring you for sex.

- *Remember that stopping just short of intercourse can have many of the same emotional results as actually having sex.* The closeness, the feeling of being aroused, can create the same emotional ties as going all the way. You can get hurt just as badly.

- *It's okay to be rude.* If the only way to say no is to yell, push, or walk away, that's what you need to do.

- *Ask God to help you resist temptation.* Prayer is a powerful weapon.

"It takes a lot more courage to stay true to yourself in this world than it takes to give in," says McClintock. "Adults have created this monster through the media and our permissive view of sex so kids have an even harder job to say no. But it's still your job."

It's hard work to say no. Trying to carry the responsibility by yourself is tough. That's why God gave you friends, parents, and adults to support you. He also gives you strength through the Holy Spirit working within you—there's "incomparably great power" in your faith.

7

Stay Alert for Hidden Dangers

Julie never thought that being alone in her friend Sara's house could be dangerous. When Julie got to Sara's house, Sara wasn't there. Knowing she'd be home soon, Julie decided to wait, even though Sara's parents had to leave. When the doorbell rang, Julie didn't see any reason not to answer the door. The three guys on the porch said they were supposed to meet Sara's older brother. Julie let them in because she knew one of them. He was her favorite teacher's son. Their families had done things together.

Julie was just a few weeks past her 13th birthday. The guys were probably 17 or 18. Julie had fun talking with them. She felt flattered that they were being so nice to her. When two of them left, leaving Julie alone with the boy she knew, she didn't suspect any trouble. But he followed her into the kitchen. That's where he raped her, on the floor.

"It wasn't a real pleasant thing," Julie says, vastly understating the pain, embarrassment, and fear she felt. Julie never told anyone about the rape. "I had so much respect for his father," she says. "I didn't want to put the families through anything. I knew it would tear apart their family as well as my own."

That was 10 years ago. "I think I just kind of blocked it," Julie says now. "I pushed it back and pushed it back. For a long time it didn't seem like a problem because I was so young. I was never in a situation like that again. But when I got older and started dating, it resurfaced. I got very nervous. I was scared to say no to anybody. I was scared that if I did, it would progress to the same thing again. To this day I'm kind of uneasy at times, although I think I'm finally dealing with it pretty well."

———

What Julie experienced is called acquaintance rape because she knew the man who raped her—he wasn't a stranger who jumped out of the bushes.

Studies show that young women have a four times greater chance of being raped by someone they know than by a stranger. In one study, 84 percent of rape victims knew their attacker. Other studies haven't reported numbers quite that high, but they do show that many women (especially those between 16 and 24, the age range most rape victims fall into) are attacked by men they know. Sometimes victims know their attackers only slightly. Sometimes they are going out with the man—then it's called date rape.

According to Nancy Kalmerton, a social worker and therapist who works with young women who have been raped, *rape* is forced sexual intercourse. "It doesn't have to be physically brutal. It doesn't have to be at gunpoint," Kalmerton adds. "It can happen any time you are put in a position where you have no way to say no. It doesn't matter who does it—stranger, acquaintance, date, or long-term boyfriend." If the woman or the man (yes, rape can happen to men too) doesn't want to have sex and is forced to, it's rape.

The law is clear. Rape is a felony, punishable by prison time. Yet rape is one of the most under-report-ed crimes. Like Julie, many victims never say anything. They carry around a load of guilt and shame, sometimes for years. Why? Probably because they believe some myths about rape.

- *Nice girls don't get raped.* "If it happened to me, I must have led him on. It must be my fault," some victims think. They don't realize it is never the victim's fault. It is *always* the fault of the rapist.

- *Girls owe sex to guys if the guys spend a lot of money on them on a date.* It's scary that a survey of junior high kids showed that 25 percent of boys and 17 percent of girls believe this lie. The money a guy spends taking a girl on a date does not entitle him to sex.

- *If a girl is wearing a sexy outfit, she's asking for it.* Wearing sexy clothes isn't smart or God-pleasing. But no matter what a girl is wearing, it doesn't excuse rape.

- *Guys can't control themselves.* It's nonsense to say guys "have" to have sex, even if the girl says no. A guy has as much control over his sexual urges as over other urges. Would it be equally okay for him to steal food because he couldn't control his urge to eat? Or to take someone's new car because he couldn't control his urge to drive it?

- *She owes it to me.* If a girl kisses a guy or lets him touch her in a sexual way, does it mean she really wants sex or she owes it to him? Kissing someone you really like is just an expression of affection. Even sexual touching—while it's not a good idea—is not an invitation to have sex.

- *The guy was drunk so it wasn't his fault.* Alcohol *is* a huge factor in acquaintance or date rape. In fact, the guy who raped Julie had been drinking. But that doesn't excuse him. People are responsible for what they do whether drunk or sober.

- *The girl was drunk so it was her fault.* Drinking (if you are under age) and getting drunk is wrong. Drinking on a date is especially risky for girls because it may blur their thinking so much that they don't know what's happening. However, the fact that a girl was drinking doesn't give a guy the right to rape her.

All of these myths, although obviously wrong, may make a girl keep quiet if she is raped. She also may be afraid that telling will cause her parents great pain. (It will, but finding out later will be even worse.) She also may fear they will blame her. (Parents sometimes believe the myths too, but they can learn the truth).

Kalmerton says young women need to understand a couple things about rape. First, it isn't sex; it's an act of violence. "It's a power issue," Kalmerton says. "It comes out of anger, not sexual excitement." A man who rapes does so because he wants to feel in charge and often because he's angry at women, not because he can't control his desire for sex.

Second, it's never the victim's fault. "A girl has the right to say no at any time," Kalmerton says. "If that no isn't respected, then the other person has gone beyond the limit." No matter what clothes you've worn or what you've done, rape isn't your fault. While women sometimes do dumb things that put them at risk for rape, that doesn't excuse the guy.

What can you do to prevent date or acquaintance rape? First a word to girls.

Kalmerton says society teaches girls things that increase their risk of being raped. For example, girls always are supposed to be polite, to flatter guys, to let them take the lead, to be passive, and not to stand up for what they think. While these values are beginning to change, Kalmerton says, the attitudes are still out there.

Society also teaches girls that their main worth is in being pretty so they can attract boys.

Neither of these is true.

As a girl you have great worth. God makes that clear. He made you. You are important for your mind, for your spirit, for who you are—not just for how you look. You have the right to your opinions and to express them. God does not want you to be passive and do whatever a guy tells you to do, especially if what he tells you is wrong. You have the right to stand up for yourself and for what you know is right.

There are some specific things you can do to lower your risk of date rape.

- *Know your limits.* Make sure the guy you are dating knows them too. God wants you to save sex for marriage. Let your date know that you believe that and are following God's plan. Learn to say no loudly, clearly, and assertively.

- *Avoid guys who put down women.* Telling sexual jokes and making insulting comments about women are signs that a guy doesn't respect women. If he doesn't respect you, he may not listen when you say no.

- *Don't go out with a guy who tries to control you.* If a guy wants to be in charge of everything, tell you what to wear or who your friends can be, run every aspect of your relationship, he may also want to "run things" sexually. You have the right to be treated as an equal. You also have a right to your opinions and a right to be respected.

- *Avoid guys who use physical power to get their way.* A guy is sending bad signals when he grabs your wrist, shoves you around, blocks you with his body, touches you when you tell him not to, or violates your personal space by moving too close for comfort.

- *Double date on blind dates or with someone you don't know well.* Don't go out alone with a guy until you have a pretty good idea of what he's like.

- *Don't go into isolated places alone with a guy.* The lake shore miles from the nearest house or the deserted woods are not good places to go on a date. Never be alone, as Julie was, with a guy you don't know well.

- *Always take money on a date.* If you have your own money, you can get home if you have to. Make a plan with your parents that if you are ever uncomfortable with a guy, you can call and they will pick you up—no questions asked.

- *Don't drink on a date or go with a guy who has been drinking.* Alcohol is probably the biggest single factor in rape. In one study of date rapists, 75 percent said they sometimes got girls drunk to make it easier to have sex with them. If you are drinking, you won't be able to think clearly—you won't sense danger signals.

- *Don't go to parties where there are no parents or adult chaperones.* Don't go off with a boy to "be alone" at any party, especially if he has been drinking. Don't go into a place where things are different from what you've been told to expect—such as into an empty house if someone told you other people would be there. Be suspicious.

- *Watch how you dress.* "It's never a girl's fault if she's raped, no matter how she's dressed," Kalmerton says, "but we do send signals by the way we dress. Your dress does have something to say about you. It's part of the impression you give. Why send a message that's confusing? Send a clear message with the way you look." Think about what message God would want you to send with your body.

Now a word to guys. Our culture also sends wrong messages to guys, which if acted upon, can lead to trouble. Society says that men are to be tough, macho, aggressive. A "real man" always gets his way, is always ready to have sex, and always has girls doing what he wants. That's a wrong message. Instead, listen to what God says about sexual responsibility and how men are to relate to women.

Remember the familiar passage about love being patient and kind, not rude or self-seeking? This refers to more than romantic love—it's Christian love, the kind God showed you in Jesus Christ. You have the privilege of living that way with others. Here are some specific guidelines.

- *Remember that God intends sex for marriage only.* Live within God's plan and you will know exactly what is God-pleasing behavior.

- *Realize that it's* never *okay to "push" a girl into sex.* No matter how long you've dated her, how much money you've spent on her, or how many times you've kissed her, it's not right to expect sex.

- *Stop when she says no.* Right away. Get rid of the idea that a girl owes you something or that she really "wants it" even though she's saying no. The idea that all women secretly want to be forced is a myth. The fact that a girl wears sexy clothes or has too much to drink is not an invitation for sex. Stop when she says no.

- *Get rid of aggressive male behavior in all areas of your life.* Don't intimidate girls by touching, pushing, or blocking them. Don't put them down by insults or raw jokes. Remember that women are your equals even though you have different roles in life. God makes that clear when He says, "There is neither ... male nor female, for you are all one in Christ Jesus" (Galatians 3:28).

- *Think about your mom or your sister.* Don't do anything to a girl that you wouldn't want done to your mom or your sister.

Now that we know some of the danger signals, what can you do if you think you're going to be raped? First, trust your instincts. If something doesn't seem quite right, don't shrug it off. Get out of there. "If you feel that something's wrong, it probably is," Julie says, looking back on her experience. "Even if it isn't, it's better to be on the safe side."

Here are some suggestions from Kalmerton and other experts on date rape.

- *Try to stay calm, hard as it may be.* No matter how strong your emotions, stay in control. Think.

- *Act right away.* Don't wait for the guy to try something a second time. Even if you think you might be misunderstanding what he's doing, don't take a chance.

- *Be assertive.* Shout "No!" or "Stop!" loudly and clearly. Pleading or crying probably won't work.

- *Run and scream for help.* If you decide to fight, do it with all your might, not halfheartedly. A self-defense course can teach you what to do, but never fight if he has a weapon.

- *Lie.* A few women have escaped being raped by telling their attacker they have AIDS or another sexually transmitted disease. As Christians, we know lying is a sin. However, in this case, it may prevent greater pain and suffering.

- *Last resort.* If you sense that your attacker is really dangerous, especially if he has a weapon, it may be better to submit than to be hurt or killed.

What should you do if you are raped?

- *Tell someone.* This is number 1. Don't keep it to yourself. Remember, it's not your fault. Tell your parents, tell a teacher or minister, call a rape crisis hotline. "I regret not telling," says Julie.

"Hard as it may be, go through with it. It's definitely better. It makes you feel it's ended."

- *Tell the police*. This may be very hard, but if your attacker gets away with it, he could do it to someone else.

- *Get medical help right away*. You need to be tested for sexually transmitted diseases or pregnancy. The police will need evidence of the rape to build a case against your attacker. Doctors and nurses at rape centers will understand what you went through and will help you through the tests.

- *Get some support*. You may need to see a counselor. Depression often follows rape, and it will be worse without support. Your family may need help in dealing with it also.

- *You can heal*. Remember, says Kalmerton, you can come through this and be able to trust again. You can regain control of your life. It is possible to heal, but don't try to do it alone.

A special word for guy victims. Girls aren't the only ones who are raped. It doesn't happen very often, but guys can be raped too. Sometimes it's by a woman. Usually it isn't by physical force but by intimidation—"You do this with me or I'm going to tell everyone that you're gay" or some other threat. That rape is no different than rape by physical force. Remember that you don't have to go along with her, no matter what she says. A loud no may make her back off.

More often, though, male rape is done by a man to a younger guy. All the things we've said about rape for girls apply just as much to guys. A guy may be afraid to tell what happened because he may be afraid that the rape makes him gay. Remember, being raped is not your fault. It doesn't mean you are a homosexual. It means you were forced by someone who is cruel and sick.

Here are a few tips from Kalmerton.

- *Be aware.* Sometimes an older man may talk a younger boy into doing something that he really doesn't understand. Know that sexual touching between a man and a boy—or having the man put his penis into any body opening—is wrong. Don't go along with it, no matter what the man promises.

- *Keep your space.* Be aware if another guy, especially an older one, is getting too close. If you feel he's getting into your personal space, or that his touching doesn't feel quite right, it probably isn't.

- *Be wary of "secrets."* When anybody says to keep something secret, watch out. There shouldn't be secrets. If you can't do something in public, then it shouldn't happen in private either.

God has a wonderful plan for His gift of sex. It never includes forcing someone to have sex.

You can't go on a date bristling with suspicion, expecting danger at every turn. That would take away all the fun. At the same time, be aware that rape does happen, and often the rapist is someone the victim knows. Stay alert, but enjoy the fun of being with other young people. That's what God intended.

8

When Adults Break the Rules

He was a new teacher, kind of cute. As a seventh grader, Marcy had him for math. She started hanging around after school to talk with him. He gave her some papers to grade. It was nice in the empty classroom, both of them working quietly. When she handed him the stack of graded papers, his smile made it all worthwhile.

One afternoon he told Marcy about how upset his wife was because he was so involved with school activities. In the next few weeks, he told her more:

how lonely he was, how his wife didn't understand him, how cold she was. Marcy was flattered that he had chosen to confide in her. She wanted to help him. At first her "helping" was just listening. Then one day, he hugged her and held her for a long time. Soon it progressed to kissing, then to sexual touching.

Marcy didn't know what to do. She knew it wasn't right, but she also really cared about her teacher. The closeness, the warmth, even the touching, felt good. How could it be wrong? Besides, if she told anyone, he'd lose his job—how could she do that to someone she liked?

———

Marcy isn't one person, she's a combination of several people. But her story is all too real for many teenagers. Some adults want to have sexual contact with kids; often they make teenagers their victims. While it happens most often to girls, it can happen to guys too.

Why does a grown-up want to have sex with a kid? "Often these are adults who have an underlying feeling of inferiority," says Dr. John Juern, a psychologist. "They don't feel they are able to attract someone in the normal way so they become interested in kids. They see them as less threatening."

These sexual abusers are not usually violent people, Dr. Juern says, although a few have beaten or even killed their victims. Usually their number 1 goal is to satisfy their sexual needs, and they don't worry about how that might affect anyone else. "They are often very self-centered people," says Dr. Juern. "They can use fear and intimidation, though, to keep the young person quiet."

There are some myths about sexual contact between adults and children that need to be replaced with facts.

- *Sex between kids and adults is always forced. If the child isn't bruised, it didn't happen.* Not true. "Mind pressure" is just as strong as physical pressure. Marcy wasn't doing the things she did because the teacher was holding a knife on her—but he was forcing her just the same.

- *Only strangers abuse children. Adults that kids know and trust don't.* Unfortunately, most sexual abuse of kids is done by someone they like and trust—a family member or relative, a teacher or youth leader, a neighbor, or a friend's family member.

- *Sexual abuse only happens to kids who hang around with a bad crowd, not to "nice" kids.* It can happen to anybody—even if you live in a nice neighborhood and go to a Christian school.

- *Christians don't do things like that.* We all wish that were true, but all people are sinners, even Christians. And Christians also can have emotional problems that may lead them to sexually abuse children.

- *The child or teen must have done something to encourage the adult.* It is never the child's fault. If it happens to you, it is not your fault. Marcy wasn't at fault even though she stayed after school, let the teacher tell her about his problems, and didn't say no when he started touching her. The teacher was using his power and authority to get her to do those things and *it was his fault.*

- *Any sexual contact with an adult means the child will never have a normal life.* Sexual abuse is a terrible thing. It can affect a person's whole life, but there are ways to recover from it. With God's help and the help of a parent or counselor, children or teens who have been sexually abused can rebuild their lives and go on to have normal adult sexual relationships.

How does a sexual relationship start between an adult and a child? Probably slowly. "It often starts with something that's not sexual. The behavior is accepted because this is a trusted person," says Dr. Juern. "It might be spending time together, appropriate touching like a pat on the back. Gradually the boundaries are worn away." The talking and sharing become more and more personal. The touching becomes more intimate. The victim may be uneasy with each new step but gradually accepts it. Before long, the victim is in so deep there doesn't seem to be any way out that won't hurt a lot of people.

Let's get something clear here: Most friends, relatives, teachers, and other adults are good people—only a tiny percentage abuse kids sexually. You don't have to be afraid that every friendly gesture is the start of sexual abuse. God made the adults in your life warm and friendly for a reason, and He wants you to enjoy their company. Don't see a child molester in every adult who hugs you! At the same time, you need to be aware of some warning signs that an adult is crossing the line. According to Dr. Juern, here are some red flags.

- A *"gut feeling" that something is wrong*. "There's no way to measure this scientifically," says Dr. Juern, "but if there's any question 'Is it okay for me to do this?' that's a pretty good clue something is wrong."

- *An adult who finds ways to be alone with you.* If he sends other kids away, asks you to come to his house alone, or asks to meet you in some isolated place, this should be a warning.

- *"Accidental" touching of private areas.* Brushing up against your body or hugs that press body parts together or last too long are not normal.

- *Sexual topics in your conversations.* Talking about sexual practices, telling sexual jokes, or showing sexual pictures isn't something adults should do with kids.

- *Confiding personal information.* Marriage and sexual problems are matters that an adult should tell another adult, not a teen.

Dr. Juern says kids who are approached sexually by an adult usually have a lot of mixed feelings. At first it feels good because they're getting attention from someone in authority, someone they like and even may be attracted to. Those positive feelings are important for the adult too. He or she uses them to wear down the victim's boundaries and get cooperation.

But as the abuse goes further, victims usually feel awkward, embarrassed, and guilty. They know they shouldn't be doing it, but they don't see how they can tell anyone. They begin to take responsibility for the abuse and feel like it's their fault.

It's not. The victim has been "set up" for this. The adult is responsible and at fault. The adult is using feelings of guilt and shame to keep the sexual contact going.

What should you do if an adult makes a sexual move on you?

- *Tell the person no loudly and clearly.* You can say simply, "I don't want to do this. It's wrong." It takes a lot of courage to say that to someone in authority, such as a teacher or relative, but remember the person is using adult authority to try to take advantage of you. Often a clear no will make the person back off and leave you alone.

- *Tell another adult.* The adult who approached you may look for another victim, someone who isn't as strong-willed as you. You have to tell someone who can stop the abuser. Your parents, another teacher, your pastor, or a relative you trust are all good choices.

What if you're currently involved in this type of abusive relationship?

- *Realize that the adult probably won't stop.* You have to find the courage to say, "This is wrong.

It has to stop." Then tell someone. Again, it takes a lot of guts to tell, but it has to be done. "It's a big burden to put on a kid," says Dr. Juern, "but you have to stop it because the adult won't."

- *Don't let liking the person stop you from talking.* You can't let fear of hurting the adult, causing the loss of a job, or causing family problems stop you from telling. You have to put yourself first. Remember, it's the adult's fault—losing a job or a marriage is not because of you, it's because of what he or she did.

Afterward you can expect to feel bad. The whole thing will not be easy. You may feel guilty because you let it go on so long. You may feel guilty because of what happened to the adult. Other adults or kids may dislike you for "causing trouble." But that's better than being a victim, and it's better than other kids being victimized after you. You may need to talk to a counselor to help you work through the feelings.

What if the adult is your parent? Sexual abuse by a parent means there are deep psychological problems. This is not something you can handle yourself. *You must get help.* Telling your other parent may not be the best place to start. The shock if he or she really didn't know—the guilt if he or she did know but was denying it—can make matters worse. Tell a teacher, a pastor, a school social worker, or an adult you trust. Let that person guide you through the emotional minefield that sexual abuse by a parent brings.

Three other important points to think about.

- *Guys and adult males.* It does not mean you are a homosexual if you have sexual contact with a man. Dr. Juern emphasizes that you were having sex because of the abuser's authority, not because it was your choice.

- *If your parents don't believe you.* Some kids have told their parents about the sexual advances of a teacher or youth leader and the parents have said, "You must be imagining it. He wouldn't do that." Don't give up. Keep telling your parents that it's true, and at the same time, tell someone else such as another teacher.

- *Lying about sexual abuse.* Some kids have lied about adults making sexual advances because they were angry at them. As a Christian, you know lying is a sin. But sexual abuse of a child is one of the worst things any adult can be accused of. It ruins lives, destroys careers, and ends marriages. If the accusation is true, then that's the price the adult must pay. If it's false, the adult may never recover. Even if he or she is found innocent, the cloud may never leave. *Never make an accusation like this if it isn't true.*

Kids who are victimized by adults may have a hard time long into the future. God tells us to forgive those who sin against us, but even if you do, you may not be able to put it behind you easily. You may think your feelings are gone, perhaps for years, and then they pop up later. "It's almost like a posttraumatic stress disorder," says Dr. Juern. "The emotions from the stressful event may come back when something triggers them because they were so strong."

That doesn't mean there's something wrong with you. Remember to place your trust in God. He will never leave you. He always will be there to help you deal with those feelings. That's why He's given you adults—parents and counselors—who can help if you give them a chance.

9

What *Are* You Listening To?

"I believe rock music is just a commercial that says 'Have sex with as many people as you can,' " says Dave, a former rock musician and rock junkie, who went to many concerts during his teen years. "It says some other things too, like 'Do drugs.' 'Don't take any lip from anybody.' 'Get money and rule the world.' "

Do you spend a lot of time listening to rock music? Most teenagers do. If you do, you probably know more about the messages in rock lyrics than your parents do! But you may choose not to think about them. After all, your friends listen to rock music, rap, and hip hop. It would be very hard to have to ask for an explanation when someone talks about the current hit song.

"It won't hurt me. I won't be influenced by it," you may say. And you may be right. Maybe you will be able to ignore the negative messages rock artists pour into your ears. No one is saying that everybody who listens to rock music jumps into bed with someone at the first chance or takes drugs or drinks too much.

You do need to think carefully about what you are doing. Listen carefully to what rock and rap artists say. Look at their lifestyles. Then ask yourself, "Would God agree with what they are telling me?"

Here's a little information to get you thinking about the messages in rock music, especially those about sex. Yes, it comes from people who are opposed to popular music—but give them a chance to speak.

"Every possible negative way of life is glorified, praised and promoted in rock music," says Rev. John Spangler, a minister who has spent years studying rock music and gives seminars on its dangers. He finds the values in rock especially bad when it comes to sex. "The word *love* in rock music means *sex*," he warns. " 'Let me love you all night long' doesn't mean 'Let's have an emotional relationship until the sun comes up!' "

Rock music says every kind of sex is okay: sex between guys and girls; sex with members of the same sex; sex with parents and brothers and sisters; rape; sex combined with torture; and sex with animals. Rap music, especially, is rough on women. "Women are shown as sex objects to be used by men, as people who like being beaten," Rev. Spangler says. Does that make you angry, girls? It should.

Sex has always been a subtle message in rock music, but in the last few years, it's become even more open. The sexual images in modern rock music are a raw, brutal punch to the face. It's hard to write about these images in a Christian book. If you've been listening to rock music, they're not new to you. If you haven't, you might be shocked. Here are just a few.

- The artist formerly known as Prince sings about 23 ways to have sex in a one-night stand—on the kitchen floor, in the bathtub, and on the pool table. The music video shows naked women led blindfolded into an orgy of squirming bodies. He praises incest in his song "Sister," saying it's everything it's said to be.

- NWA, in "Findum, F——um and Flee," sings in street language about sex organs raw from intercourse and orders to the "bitch" for oral sex. (Women in rap songs are routinely referred to as either "bitch" or "ho" meaning whore.)

- Rapper Ice-T sings, "Let's get butt naked and f——."

MTV is the perfect outlet for modern music that pushes sex because visual images combined with the lyrics are more powerful than words alone. A researcher at Michigan State University found that watching just one hour of MTV per day will expose the viewer to 1,500 sex experiences every year. For example, Janet Jackson's love song may have mild words, but the image of her in lacy underwear with a man stroking and kissing her body isn't mild at all.

"The clothes they wear, the positions they assume, the kinds of sexual activity the videos suggest is horrendous," says Rev. Spangler. "I think they have a lot of responsibility for the spread of sexually transmitted diseases and teen pregnancy because the songs and videos are designed to turn you on."

Dave agrees. "If young teens who never had sex are dancing to this music and thinking about doing it, the music gives them permission," he says.

A lot of rock artists don't hide their own sex lives. They brag about the groupies that follow them. They boast about their sexual activities with them. Most band members don't bother with marriage. If they do, it usually doesn't last long. They're not exactly great role models for happy family life.

And after they've convinced kids to have sex, rock artists are right there to push abortion. Some musicians belong to an organization called "Rock for Choice," which knows how to influence kids. One female singer, talking about abortion, said in a magazine interview, "[When kids see] people they really respect and love speaking out on this issue, it becomes part of the experience, and they accept it with the music." A female guitarist said in the same interview, "We didn't want to preach to the converted. We wanted to get people who would be affected by abortion laws the most: young kids."

Sex isn't the only thing rock music pushes. There are also strong images of violence. "They're singing about beating to a pulp anyone who doesn't agree with you," Dave explains.

Grammy-nominee Suicidal Tendencies has a song called "I Saw Your Mommy and Your Mommy's Dead," which describes chopped off feet and rats nesting in her hair. The gangsta rap group The Geto

Boys sings about getting a girl "ready and sweaty" and then slicing her up with a machete until her guts are like spaghetti. Guns 'n Roses has a song titled "I Used to Love Her But I Had to Kill Her." The name Iron Maiden comes from a spike-studded body case used for torture. One of the group's album covers shows a band member hacking someone with a bloody axe.

Violence in rock has reached new heights on MTV. The National Coalition on Television Violence analyzed the content of 750 music videos and found they averaged more than 20 violent acts per hour. Just one example: The video for "Poundcake" by Van Halen shows a group of women using a power drill to drill out the eye of someone watching through a keyhole.

The violent image some rock groups portray on stage and in videos can spill over into their personal lives. Several rappers and rock stars have been arrested for violent behavior such as murder, car jacking, and physical abuse. Because kids can have trouble separating the image and the music, some concertgoers have lost control and turned some concerts into riots.

As if sex and violence weren't enough, rock music promotes the drugs and drinking that fuel the fire.

Use of any kind of chemical is glorified by rock groups. You never see Axl Rose of Guns 'n Roses without a bottle of whiskey in his hand. Rumor has it that the alcohol bottles on stage are really full of herbal tea, but even if that's true, it doesn't excuse pushing alcohol to fans under legal drinking age.

Rock songs are filled with drug references, but they have become more hidden. When a group sings about Panama, did you know that's marijuana? Or that Mr. Brownstone is heroin? Some kids know this. Others sing along without any idea of what they're saying.

The lifestyles of rock musicians are too often an advertisement for drugs and alcohol. Many rock stars are known users, many have been through treatment. Recently, several popular alternative rock musicians have died from drug overdoses. That doesn't seem to stop groups such as KISS from singing songs such as "Mr. Speed" or "Mainline" (about injecting drugs) or a group with the biblical-sounding name Nazareth from doing a song titled "Cocaine."

As you can guess from the lyrics, some rock groups don't like God or religion. After all, Christ speaks out loudly and clearly against what the bands appear to stand for. As a result, they tear down anything that has to do with Christ or the Christian church—the Bible, Christian symbols, and the clergy. For example, the group Slayer sings, "I can take your lost soul from the grave/Jesus knows your soul cannot be saved/Crucify the so-called Lord." George Michael, in his album misnamed "Faith," sings that he doesn't need the Bible, just sex. Or Ozzy Osbourne smashes a cross to the floor.

If some rock artists hate Christianity, others like Satan. These bands' album covers are filled with occult symbols, and many songs glorify Satan. Maybe only a few rock artists practice satanism and the rest just hint at it to boost sales, but that doesn't excuse any of them. "If they only emphasize Satan for money, that's the worst reason of all," says Rev. Spangler. "They don't care how it's affecting kids—kids who take them seriously even if they're not."

There's one last evil that rock music promotes—suicide. The rate of suicide among teens has skyrocketed more than 300 percent in the last 20 years. Suicide is one of the leading causes of death among high school students. When you count the deaths officially listed as car accidents or drug overdoses that might not be accidental, suicide could leap to number 1. Many psychologists support rock groups that say music can't cause a person to commit suicide. And certainly we can't prove that it does. We can, however, say that if you are depressed, you easily can find the message in rock music that suicide is okay and will solve your problems. "People who are looking for permission to blow themselves away will hear it in rock music," says Rev. Spangler.

Elton John sings about buying a .45 and giving them all a surprise. "Think I'm gonna kill myself, cause a little suicide," he sings. The alternative band Nirvana sang the song "I Hate Myself and Want to Die." The group's lead singer, Kurt Cobain, killed himself with a shotgun.

Even if music doesn't cause kids to kill themselves, common sense has to ask if it's healthy to listen to music that pours death messages into your mind. At this point, you have to ask yourself some questions.

- *What's God's plan?* Does rock music promote sex that's outside God's plan? Does it promote drug and alcohol use? violence? satanism? Does it give false messages about death and suicide? Compare the lyrics and God's Word.

- *Can this music hurt me?* If I listen to this stuff, will I be harmed? Even if I don't run out and do the things rock music is promoting, am I exposing myself to destructive messages?

84

- *Who gets rich?* If I buy this CD, am I putting money into the pockets of people who promote sinful, destructive lifestyles?

- *What do I do?* If the answer to these questions is yes, what does God—who sent His Son to die in payment for the sins rock music promotes—want me to do?

Turning away from rock music, especially if you listen to it a lot, will leave a hole in your life. You need to find something to take its place. Fortunately, there's decent secular rock music out there—you just have to look for it. There's also a whole world of Christian rock. No matter what kind of music you like—top 40, heavy metal, rap—there's a Christian group doing it. And they're good—often better than the secular groups. Some Christian groups are even being played on secular radio stations. (By the way, be careful with names. A few secular groups have Christian-sounding names. For example, Ministry isn't a Christian group.)

There are even Christian rock concerts with the same excitement and high-quality entertainment the secular groups offer without the drugs, sex, and violence.

Dave has really walked through the valley of rock. "It took me to the bottom," he says. "I've done just about everything imaginable, and I've hurt a lot of people in the process. I'm very honest and open about that because I want people to learn from me."

The world of rock led Dave into both drugs and alcohol. He's been through treatment three times. He's getting his life together again and going back to school. He wants to compose, perform, and teach. "As I grow more knowledgeable, I can see the bad messages in rock," Dave says. "Those guys are very smart. They're good at their music, and they know what they're doing. But kids who follow the lifestyle they push are giving up everything, and that's why it's so horrible."

10

Dodge the Potholes
of Peer Pressure

Katie thought it was cool that her algebra teacher was out sick. High school algebra was hard, and it was good to have a break. It was even cooler when the sub left to make a phone call and told the class to study while she was gone. It wasn't so cool when one of the kids went into the teacher's desk and found a copy of the test they were going to take the next day—with the answers.

The test, of course, got passed around the room. Everybody made notes, then the student put the test back in the desk. Katie left class wondering what to do. "I talked to my friends and my boyfriend about it," she says. "They all said I shouldn't do anything, that I should just ignore it. But I couldn't do that. Later in the day, without telling anyone, I told the guidance counselor what happened."

The next day Katie's algebra teacher returned. She was angry and told the class they were getting a different—and harder—test. Katie didn't tell anyone that she'd been the one to tell, but somehow the class figured it out. Kids have a way of doing that.

"I wasn't real popular with those kids after that," Katie remembers. "There were some rough people in the class, and although they didn't directly threaten me, they made it pretty uncomfortable for a while." At least the kids who were mad at Katie weren't close friends. She admits now, several years later, that if it had been her best friends, the decision would have been even harder.

"No matter who it is—and it's going to be really tough in some cases—you have to look at yourself and your morals, at what you've been taught and what the Bible says about right and wrong," Katie says. "You have to make a stand and do what God wants. Friends come and go. They aren't always a lasting thing, but your future is."

Katie points out that cheating might not physically hurt anybody, but if you give in on one thing, you open a door. You can be pressured to do the next thing and the next. "If the pressure is for drugs or drinking or joyriding, you could be dead," she says.

———

What kids have to do to be accepted by other kids has been a problem for a long time. It's called peer pressure. It was a problem for your mom and dad when they were in school too. It's a problem for you now, and it probably isn't going to change in the future. What kids push their friends to do may change, but the pressure doesn't.

Rev. Bruce Harrmann, a counselor and religion teacher at a Christian high school, thinks today's high school social scene is different from what it was just a few years ago. "Kids cross very easily from one group to another now, more than in the past," he says. "You used to have a group that was known as the 'good kids,' but there's much more blending between groups now. Sometimes you can't count on the 'good kids' to be good. They may not want to be part of traditional morals and values anymore. The whole concept of good and bad has been so watered down in teen society."

"I think peer pressure today is subtle," adds Judy

Pretzel, a guidance counselor at the same school. "Kids test other kids. They want to find out what they're made of. And kids watch very closely to see what the group they want to be in is doing. They try to copy them so they will be seen as just like the group members. That's okay within reason in things like dress and hair styles, but copying some other things isn't."

What kind of "things" are you likely to be pressured to do in high school? That, of course, depends on the school. It can differ from group to group, but there are some pressures that seem to be common. Almost immediately we think of the pressures to try drinking, drugs, and sex. We've got whole chapters on those topics, so let's talk about some other pressures.

Here, according to Pretzel and Rev. Harrmann, are some of the pressures you can expect to find in high school.

- *Pressure to be friends with only certain people.* There are always a few leaders in every group who decide what is and isn't okay. Often they say, "If you are in our group, you can't be friends with that person." That's too bad. If you stick to your group's rigid rules, you could miss knowing interesting kids you'd really like. Sometimes kids find out the friends they hung out with when school started aren't the ones they have the most in common with.

- *Pressure to never say anything is wrong.* "You can sit at the cafeteria table with six friends. Two of them are having sex. Two are doing drugs. Two are planning to run away from home. But you are all friends, and you're not allowed to say anything they're doing is wrong," says Rev. Harrmann. This pressure reflects today's adult society where everyone is urged to be "tolerant" and calling a sin a sin is "judgmental." God does tell us to not judge others, but that doesn't mean He wants us to be quiet when friends are doing something harmful or sinful. You have to be careful to attack the sin and not the sinner, but there are times when you need to stand up and say something is wrong.

- *Pressure not to tell.* This is what Katie ran up against. Often the group says, "You don't have to do what we do to be accepted, but you better not tell." This pressure can be hard to handle by yourself, especially if the group is doing something dangerous or illegal. You may need advice from an adult. Sometimes an adult can take over, letting you off the hook. Even if the group finds out and drops you, think about what could have happened if no one stopped them. It is possible to save someone's life by *not* keeping quiet.

- *Pressure to give and take insults.* Rev. Harrmann says that many high school kids, especially guys, insult or mock each other in ways that can be very painful. Maybe it's become part of life for kids because TV characters insult one another all the time. Whatever the reason, Rev. Harrmann says you have to be able to take it and dish it out. You have to develop a thick skin to not be hurt by the insults, and you have to learn where the line is and not go too far. It can be like walking a tightrope, Rev. Harrmann says.

- *Pressure to look right but to pretend that looks don't matter.* There's an odd double standard in many high schools, Rev. Harrmann says. Kids pay lip service to the idea that people shouldn't be judged on their looks but on who they are. Underneath, though, there's still a lot of pressure to dress "right" and wear your hair the way everyone else does. Kids still decide who is "in" and "out" by how they look. Maybe the fact that kids are starting to say that looks shouldn't be so important is the first step to get rid of the beautiful-is-better standard.

These are some of the pressures you may face in high school. But it isn't enough to know they're coming. You need some ways to handle them. Here are some suggestions from Katie, Rev. Harrmann, and Pretzel.

- *Value yourself.* Value the fact that you are a much-loved child of God. "I see too many kids not valuing themselves, not valuing their bodies, not valuing their uniqueness," says Pretzel. It's hard to be unique in a teen world that pushes everyone to be the same, but God tells us we are unique. He valued us so much He sent His Son to die for us. Should we value ourselves any less?

- *Don't be too quick to jump into a group.* Sometimes kids are so anxious to be accepted that they join the first group that's willing to absorb them. Take a little time. Get to know a lot of people. Decide which group has the same morals and values as you.

- *Don't be afraid to be different in ways that count.* There are lots of harmless ways you can be like the group—dress, hairstyle, music. But when it comes to morals and values, you may need to be different. And that may not be all negative.

When you do take a stand—especially if you fit into the group in other ways—kids may see you as a leader. "There might be something that goes off in their brains that says, 'Hey, he had the courage to say no, what's going on here?'" says Pretzel. They could end up agreeing with you.

- *Don't base your values on what other kids think.* It's hard to realize now, but where you fit into the high school social scene has little to do with how successful you will be later. Sometimes the "high school stars" never grow up beyond that—and the "out-of-it" ones become leaders.

- *Find friends who have the same values.* It's easier to take a stand if you've got somebody to support you. Even if it's just one friend, you can help each other say no.

- *Keep a strong, open relationship with your parents.* They can offer support and advice because they may have gone through some of the same struggles. Find a quality teacher you can talk to. He or she will understand the social situation in your particular school and can help guide you through the minefield.

- *Develop a strong relationship with your Lord.* "Pray

about it," Katie says. "God's not going to leave you alone. He may be testing you to strengthen your faith." And God's Word promises that He'll never test you beyond what you can endure.

Sharon Scott, who worked with a police department as a counselor for kids in trouble, developed a plan for dealing with peer pressure. In her book *PPR: Peer Pressure Reversal*, she says you should do these things when you feel pressured into something.

- *Check out the scene.* Look and listen carefully to what's going on around you.

- *Apply the "trouble rule."* It asks two questions: Does it break a law? Will it make anybody in authority (for Christian kids, that includes God) angry? If the answer to either question is yes, you need to resist.

- *Act to avoid trouble.* Acting, of course, is the hardest part. But Scott offers some specific suggestions.

- *Say no.* You don't have to give an excuse, just look the person in the eye and level with him or her. You can phrase no in different ways: "I'll take a pass." "Sorry, Charlie!" "No way!" "Not if

I want to stay alive." "Forget it." "Not in this lifetime." You can probably think of many more. The key is your answers should all say no loudly and clearly.

- *Just leave.* "I'm outta here!" The sight of your back as you go through the door sends an unmistakable message!

- *Make an excuse.* Here's where parents can come in handy—"My parents would kill me" puts the blame on them. Some other excuses include "I promised to baby-sit that night." "I'm grounded so I can't go." "I've gotta work that night." "Drinking makes me break out." Excuses can get you off the hook, but remember, they don't address the real issue of saying something is wrong.

- *Make a joke.* Kids admire a sense of humor. Use a flip remark to get out of a trouble situation. "I'd love to go, but I've got to go home and brush my dog's teeth." "Alcohol makes my hair turn green." "I promised my plants we'd have an in-depth discussion tonight." Put your imagination to work—the more off-the-wall, the better.

- *Act shocked.* You might make the other person

stop and think if you say something like: "I can't believe you said that." "You couldn't possibly mean that." "What a goofy idea." "Are you *crazy?*" or "Earth calling Chris." That gives your friend a way out by saying, "I was just joking."

- *Flatter the person.* "You're too smart to really mean that." "You're too important to me to let you do that." "You usually have such good ideas." "I really like you, and I want to stay friends, but I'm not doing that."

- *Offer an alternative.* "Let's go swimming instead." "I'd rather go to a movie." "Why don't we see what Mike and Sue are doing?" Then if your friend continues on the wrong track, you can say, "Well, I'm doing this instead."

"God created you to be an individual, but He has also put you in a very social world," Pretzel sums up. "He wants you to have friends and to be a friend." But sometimes you'll have to go against what friends want.

"That's not easy," Katie says. "But hard as is it, you have to look at what God tells you and make that stand."

11

Living under the Influence

Devon was very young when he first tried alcohol—8 or 9 years old. He'd slug down what was left in the bottom of glasses left by his hard-drinking father and mother. They never noticed. As his home life got more chaotic, Devon found ways to escape. By the time he was 11, escape meant having a beer. When he was in fifth grade, he got drunk for the first time at the home of an adult friend. "He gave me beer, trying to treat me like an adult, I guess," Devon remembers. That man didn't do Devon any favor.

By the time he was in junior high, Devon and his friends were getting drunk before basketball games. "I really liked it," he says. "I never got sick from drinking." (Maybe it would have been better if he had.)

Instead Devon got in deeper. First, he stole a few inches from the liquor bottles in his parents' cabinet. Then, he had his buddy's older sister swipe six-packs from the service station where she worked.

When Devon started high school, he also started experimenting with other drugs. Finally, he couldn't hide his drinking and drug use from his teachers. He went through drug and alcohol treatment for the first time in ninth grade.

———

Unfortunately, Devon's story isn't unusual. There's an epidemic of alcohol and drug use by U.S. teenagers.

According to a 1995 survey by the University of Michigan Institute for Social Research, 81 percent of teens said they've used alcohol at some point in their lives. An earlier study by the National Institute on Alcohol Abuse and Alcoholism showed that between a quarter and a third of high school seniors have an alcohol problem. More than a third of high school seniors say their friends get drunk at least once a week. A survey done by *Weekly Reader* said a third of *fourth* graders were feeling peer pressure to try alcohol and 70 percent of eighth graders have tried it. Three in five teens said they drink at least once a month; one in four drinks at least once a week; and many have five drinks or more at one time (binge drinking) at least once a week.

Drug use by teens is also climbing. While rates went down during the 1980s, they are now skyrocketing. According to the University of Michigan survey, almost half of high school seniors have used an illegal drug at least once. The percentage of eighth graders using drugs almost doubled between 1991 and 1995. Marijuana use showed the biggest increase, followed by LSD, amphetamines, stimulants, and inhalants. Cocaine and heroin use, while small by comparison to other drugs, also went up.

That's an interesting bunch of statistics, you may say, but what do I *really* need to know about alcohol and drugs?

First, you need to know that alcohol is indeed a drug. "Alcohol is a drug because it's a mood- or mind-altering substance, just like many others," says Gabriele Pfoh, an alcohol and drug counselor who works with kids. "Drugs all work in a very similar way, even though you put them into the body in different ways. All of them work in the brain. All of them get there through the bloodstream. And all of them affect every organ in the body."

Drugs affect the body in different ways, Pfoh says. Some are "uppers"; some are "downers"; some make you hallucinate. But all drugs mess with the chemicals in your brain and prevent messages from getting from brain cell to brain cell quickly and clearly. That's why thinking and reaction times slow when you are drunk or high. It's also why you can black out and not remember what happened when you come to.

Knowing why kids use drugs can give you some clues about how to avoid them. Devon thinks the biggest reason he drank was to have friends. "It gives you a crowd of people," he says. "It gives you something to do with other kids where you're all in the same boat. It makes you feel like no one's going to leave you and everything is fine." Devon doesn't think most kids really like the feeling of being drunk, but "they like being drunk with a bunch of people."

Devon says he couldn't have told his friends that he was going to stop drinking and still stay friends. There was too much pressure to be one of the gang. Without drinking, he would have been on the outside.

Pfoh agrees that peers are a major influence. She also sees a couple of other reasons kids use alcohol or other drugs.

- *The need to feel better.* There are pressures in adolescence—family problems, lack of self-confidence, adjusting to normal body changes, pressure to perform in school or sports. Whatever the pressure, some kids use alcohol or other drugs to cope.

- *The need to have fun.* Some teens drink to celebrate. Your team won—get drunk!

- *The need to feel grown up.* Adults drink so if I drink, I must be grown up.

- *The need to rebel.* Kids know that their parents (and society in general) don't approve of teen drinking. Doing it makes them feel a little wild, a little rebellious. Unfortunately that "little rebellion" can escalate into major problems.

- *The easy availability.* Alcohol is legal for adults and easy for teens to buy, even if they're underage. Drugs also are easily bought in almost every high school.

- *The glamor.* Alcohol and drugs seem to be glamorized in movies, rock music, and on TV. Some kids really do think that everybody is doing it and it's cool.

On TV and in the movies, using alcohol can

look like fun. Even the slang words for being drunk—trashed, wasted, blasted, bombed—have a feeling of something adventurous.

The reality is different.

First, alcohol and other drugs affect your sense of judgment. "You might not normally dance on tables," says Pfoh, "but if you have a few beers, especially if you haven't built up any tolerance, you can lose your sense of restraint. You may do things you would not normally do. After the alcohol has worn off, you can be very embarrassed. 'Oh, did I really do that?' Sometimes you may not even remember. It's a scary thing when you're missing a few hours of your life."

Pfoh also warns that getting drunk often leads to experimenting with sex. "Alcohol inhibits what is planted inside us by the teachings of parents, family, church, school, the Bible," she says. "Their voices can become fainter and fainter. Alcohol can be a powerful releaser of the pleasure seeker within us—the part that says, 'I don't care, I just want what I want, here and now.' "

In her work with teens, Pfoh has heard many stories about young men and women who got drunk and did some stupid things—such as having sex. "You can end up acting on values that are not your own," she warns. "You can wake up the next morning realizing you did something that was not right and you can feel ashamed and guilty." You risk getting pregnant, getting someone pregnant, or getting a sexually transmitted disease. Alcohol also plays a huge role in date rape.

Sex is only one danger of drinking or doing drugs. Another danger is drunk teens who get into cars. Last year in my city, a teenage girl who had just graduated from high school drove her car full speed into a tree after a graduation party. Her graduation was the last big event in her life.

Emergency room doctors and nurses can tell you about another danger. Too much alcohol, especially in a body that's not used to it, can cause alcohol poisoning. The victim passes out, goes into a coma, and dies. Many drugs have the same fatal consequences. Cocaine can cause an instant heart attack. Sniffing inhalants can cause permanent brain damage or quick death from suffocation.

Even if you survive in the short run, long-term use of alcohol or other drugs can lead to a variety of physical and mental problems. Addiction is a very real disease, and one that's hard to overcome. Devon has been through treatment three times. Every time he thinks he's conquered it, something happens to send him back to using—his girlfriend leaves or his old drinking and drug buddies pressure him. Untreated addiction leads to a wasted life and physical breakdown. It costs addicts their education, job, family, self-worth, the people they love, and finally life itself.

The best way to avoid problems with alcohol and drugs is to stay away from them in the first place. That means not using alcohol until you are of legal age and then never overusing it. It means not using illegal drugs at all. Ever.

Following that plan means you will have to use a certain word a lot—no.

How can you make it as easy on yourself as possible? Here are some suggestions from Pfoh and Devon.

- *Learn about alcohol and drugs.* Don't depend on just the information in this short chapter. Do some reading. Books in your public library can tell you about the risks of drinking and doing other drugs in much greater detail. Listen to speakers who may visit your school. Talk to counselors at school and church. Use the information to make a really educated decision about your own attitude toward alcohol and drug use.

- *Treat your body carefully.* Think through what God has told you about respecting your body. He only gives you one. How you treat it is your responsibility and privilege.

- *Learn about the law.* Drinking when you are under age or using drugs at any age is illegal. If the police raid a party where there is drinking or drug use, they won't ask if you were actually using. If kids have an accident after drinking at your house, their parents can sue your parents. Your family could lose everything they've worked for.

- *Have fun.* Remember, it's a myth that you only have fun at a party if there's drinking. Most people who drink too much end up throwing up. Is that your idea of fun? Find a group of friends who know how to have fun without drinking or drugs. Have a blast with them.

- *Remember the sexual risks.* Consider how alcohol and drugs can affect your feelings about sex. Think about how that could affect your decision to wait to have sex until marriage. Think about the risks that teen sex brings.

- *Build a support group.* Find one or two good friends who agree with you about not drinking or taking drugs. It's easier to say no, or to leave a place where kids are drinking and getting high, if you don't have to do it alone. A couple of friends who can say, "Remember, we said we weren't going to do that. Let's go!" can be a big help.

- *Plan to go home*. Make a pact with your parents that if you ever call and say you want to come home, they will pick you up without any questions. You might arrange a code word that means "There's drinking or drugs here and I want out." Always carry enough money to make a phone call or to take a taxi home if you can't reach your parents.

- *Know your date*. Be sure of the standards of your date. You may not be able to change his or her opinions. You might ask, "Does this person want to do things I don't want to do?" If the answer is yes, you may have to end the relationship.

- *Stay active*. Fill your life with things that are fun: sports, drama, music. Find your friends through these activities. Fill your time with them to reduce the temptation to fill it with drinking and drugs.

- *Pray.* Remember that God's strength is there for you to tap.

- *Be willing to walk alone.* That's Devon's final word of advice. "You have to learn to be alone," he says. "You can't always worry if people are going to be there. If you can walk your own path, people will follow. Think about Bible people like Joseph and Daniel. They had to walk alone sometimes. You have to be able to say, '*No one* is going to get me into alcohol or drugs.' When kids see that kind of strength, they respond to it. And you will have friends."

The Most Common Drugs and Their Effects

- *Alcohol.* Beer, wine, and wine coolers are teen favorites. Alcohol is a depressant. It slows the brain and central nervous system. Drinking causes poor judgment and coordination, and it can cause emotional outbursts and aggression. It's a factor in many teen deaths from car crashes, other accidents, fights, and acute alcohol poisoning. It often leads to sex, which can result in pregnancy or sexually transmitted diseases. It's also a big factor in date rape.

- *Marijuana.* It is most often smoked but sometimes eaten in food. It's a central nervous system depressant that causes hallucinations. Some people experience panic reactions when using it. Long-term use causes poor memory, extreme sleepiness, and lowered ability to have sex. It also may cause lung cancer.

- *Inhalants.* They are especially popular among teens because they are cheap, legal, and give a quick high. Kids sniff solvents, glue, gasoline, lighter fluid, typewriter correction fluid, and just about any type of aerosol. The stuff is usually sprayed into a plastic bag and breathed in. It acts as a central nervous system depressant, giving a feeling of being drunk along with dreamlike hallucinations that last from 15 minutes to several hours. Brain damage is a big risk, along with lung, liver, and kidney damage, and burning out the nose and lungs. Kids have died from heart failure or suffocation while sniffing.

- *Cocaine*. It looks like powdered sugar and can be sniffed or smoked. Crack, a pastelike form of cocaine that's hardened into small rocklike balls, is one of the most addictive substances in the drug world. Cheap and easily available, it can hook a person after just a few uses. A central nervous system stimulant, cocaine causes the user to breathe fast and his or her heart to pound. It can cause heart attacks and strokes in otherwise healthy young people.

- *LSD.* Some people think LSD is a '60s "hippy" drug that isn't currently a problem. Not so. LSD is making a comeback. Sold in tablets or on sheets of paper, LSD causes hallucinations, which can be dangerous. Some users have thought they could fly and jumped off roofs. The hallucinations don't always go away when the drug wears off. People who have taken LSD have had mental breakdowns. They may experience flashbacks months or years after they've taken the drug. Terribly dangerous, LSD is growing in popularity with teens who are looking for excitement.

12

Handling the
Curves in the Road

Time passes by,
Minute by minute, hour by hour,
As I see myself die.
No one around to relieve my loneliness.
No one around me who cares.
Each day that passes
I see nothing but conflicts.
No meaning to life
Yet no meaning to death.
But all inside
I see myself die.

This picture of depression was written by a 17-year-old who was seeing a counselor.

———

Teenagers get depressed. Family troubles, boyfriend or girlfriend problems, not making the basketball team, flunking a physics test—there are a bunch of things in teen life that can be depressing.

But that's not the kind of depression the poem is talking about. While the problems we've listed can be painful, for a person who is already depressed any one item could be the last straw, triggering a suicide attempt. But most kids going through a bad time know it's temporary and they'll come out the other side. They don't sink into a permanent black hole or think about ending their lives.

But some do.

Every year, 100,000 young people under the age of 24 try to kill themselves; 5,000 succeed. That's triple the rate of 30 years ago. Suicide is rising fastest among younger people: From 1980 to 1992, the suicide rate went up 28 percent among kids age 15 to 19 and a *128 percent* among kids age 10 to 14.

Not every person who is depressed tries to commit suicide, but almost all people who kill themselves are depressed. Some things in a person's background put him or her at higher risk for depression and suicide. Read this list carefully. Do many of the things apply to you? Do they apply to a friend? If your answer is yes, you or your friend could be at higher risk for depression.

- *History.* Do you have a family member or close friend who has been depressed or tried to commit suicide?

- *Family.* Is your whole family sort of depressed? Some families are always blue. It might be inherited or it could be that a depressed parent never got help.

- *Chemical abuse.* Do you use drugs and alcohol? Depression can happen when the chemicals in your brain get out of whack. Drugs and alcohol can make it worse. They can also cause aggressive, angry feelings or cause you to make poor decisions.

- *Uncertainties.* Are you unsure where you fit into the sexual world? Do you feel unattractive or awkward around the opposite sex? Are you afraid of sexual feelings or that you might be a homosexual?

- *Change.* Have you had a change in your family life, especially divorce or a parent getting remarried?

- *Stress.* Are you feeling stress that you don't think you can handle—school pressure, a romance breaking up, not making the play, being rejected by your friends?

- *Aggression.* Are you often violent or aggressive? Do you do dangerous things? Do you have brushes with the law? One study showed that teens with overly aggressive behavior had the highest chance of trying suicide.

- *Passive.* Are you shy and isolated from other kids? Is it difficult to let yourself go or have fun?

- *Examples.* Do you have a favorite rock star, movie star, or writer who has been depressed or tried suicide? Do you admire that person for what he or she did? Do you spend a lot of time listening to rock music that focuses on death—or reading about death and suicide?

There's one other risk factor that I want to give a whole paragraph, not just a few lines. It's that important.

- *Have you ever been raped or abused sexually by a friend, relative, date, teacher or other person in authority, or a stranger?* If you have, especially if you've never told anybody, you have a much higher risk of depression. One study showed that almost 25 percent of teenage girls who try suicide have been sexually abused. Statistics also show a much higher risk of depression and suicide when a teenager gets pregnant or has an abortion.

How do you tell the difference between a "down time" and a true depression in yourself or in a friend? That's not an easy question to answer. Sometimes even the experts have a hard time. But there are some signs you can look for.

- Have you lost interest in your usual activities?

- Has there been a change in your appetite? Have you gained or lost weight?

- Has there been a change in your sleep pattern? Do you experience insomnia or sleep a lot during the day?

- Do you have a loss of energy? Do you feel listless? Are you too tired to do anything?

- Are you doing drugs or alcohol?

- Do you blame yourself for everything that goes wrong, whether that's realistic?

- Do you have a low self-image, always thinking how bad or dumb or ugly you are?

- Do you feel sad, hopeless, constantly worried? Do you think your problems can't be solved?

- Do you have trouble concentrating or paying attention?

- Do you feel angry, show aggressive behavior, do dangerous stunts? Or, do you feel like you want to withdraw, hide under the covers, and never come out?

- Do you feel restless, like you can't settle down?

- Do you have a lot of physical aches and pains?

- Is your schoolwork going downhill? Are your grades dropping? Do you skip school or skip classes when you are there?

- Do you think a lot of morbid thoughts? Are you fascinated with songs, poems, or stories about death? Do you draw pictures or symbols about it?

- Do you spend a lot of time daydreaming about killing yourself? Have you begun to plan—even half-joking—about how, when, and where you would do it?

- Have you ever done something—no matter how minor—to hurt yourself?

- Do you say or think things like "I can't take it anymore" or "You'd be better off without me"?

- Do you want to give away your most valued stuff such as clothes, CDs, or pets?

- Has something awful happened—breaking up with a girlfriend or boyfriend, getting arrested, not making a team?

If you've answered yes to more than a few of these questions, you or your friend may be in a serious depression. If you are really depressed, especially if you are thinking about suicide, what should you do?

Debra Reid, a Christian counselor who works with teenagers, says the most important thing is to talk. "If you feel like you are at the end of your rope, or if you are really thinking about suicide, you have to go to someone," she says. "Talk to your parents if you possibly can. If you can't, talk to another trusted adult." That might be a grandparent, aunt or uncle, a teacher, a counselor at your school, or your pastor. Talk to one of your friends—you can get a lot of support from another teen.

Above all, be willing to talk to a professional— a doctor or psychologist. If you are seriously depressed, you may need that kind of help. There are medicines that can break the cycle of depression and help you feel good again, but only a doctor can give you a prescription.

Listen if a friend tells you that he or she thinks you are depressed. "Depression can paralyze you emotionally and take away your ability to make judgments," Reid says. "You may not realize you are depressed. Take it seriously if someone tells you that you're acting depressed."

Sometimes Christian kids don't want to admit they're depressed because they think Christians should never have problems. That's not true. Christians and Christian families can have the same problems as any family. God gives us help in coping with problems, but He never promised that we wouldn't have any. Remember that as a Christian, you have God's promise of help and support and the power of prayer to help get you through.

What if it's a friend that you're worried about? One teen can be a big help to another, so here are some things you can do.

- *Don't panic.* But at the same time, trust your instincts. If you think something is going on, it probably is.

- *Never ignore a threat or a verbal warning, even if you think your friend is just kidding.*

- *Be extra careful if your friend has just had a serious loss.* The death of a parent, the suicide of a friend, breaking up with a boyfriend or girlfriend, not making a team, or flunking a course can be the "last straw" before a suicide attempt.

- *Show your support.* Let your friend know you care and you don't want him or her to do anything harmful.

- *Tell your friend that he or she doesn't have to be miserable.* Unhappiness is not normal. There are ways to make life better. Sometimes kids think that everyone feels depressed.

- *If there's anything dangerous around, such as drugs or guns, take it away.*

- *Don't leave your friend alone.*

- *Get help right away.* You *can't* handle this alone. Don't feel ashamed for your friend or try to keep it a secret. Depression is a sickness—a temporary sickness—and nothing to be ashamed of.

- *If it's not a life-threatening emergency, get your friend to talk.* Ask direct questions like: "Are you thinking about suicide?" "Have you done anything about it?" Show your friend that there are better ways to solve problems than suicide. Tell him or her that suicide is a permanent solution to a temporary problem.

- *If it is a life-threatening emergency (your friend has done something harmful or is trying to) and you can't reach his or her parents, take your friend to an emergency room.*

According to Reid, there are a few things you should *not* do.

- *Never promise that you won't tell anyone, especially your friend's parents.* "It's too important that the teen get help. Losing trust for a while is better than losing a life," Reid points out.

- *Don't appear shocked or panicked.* It's hard, but your friend needs you to stay calm.

- *Don't judge your friend.* "This is not the time to quote the Bible about the morals of suicide," Reid says. Instead, talk about God's love. Even better, show it. Be the most loving, supportive, nonjudging friend you can be.

If one of your friends or family members commits suicide, it's important that you know what God says. Rev. Harold Senkbeil, who has dealt with several suicides, says he always thinks of Martin Luther's view of suicide. He said, "Suicide is like getting jumped in an alley."

"It isn't always done on purpose. It's often just being overpowered by things," Rev. Senkbeil says. "We can't assume that God is going to automatically condemn everybody who commits suicide. We have to remember both the Law and the Gospel."

Depression is not a hopeless illness. It's just the opposite, according to Reid. "There absolutely is hope," she emphasizes. Depression can be helped with therapy and sometimes with medication.

"The sooner you deal with depression, the better," Reid says. "The deeper you get into the hole, the harder it can be to climb out. The good news about teenage depression is that you're at the top of the hole—you haven't gone down too far."

The biggest block to getting help, Reid says, is fear. "Some people are so paralyzed by fear, they do nothing. They think if they don't talk about it, it'll go away," she says.

But it won't. Standing up to the depression and getting help is the only answer.

"God is our refuge and strength, an ever-present help in trouble" (Psalm 46:1). God loves you with an everlasting love. He is faithful. Write this on your mind and heart as you follow His road map through your teenage years. You have a guide and companion who will walk with you and help you carry the load.